Hey, kids!
See if you can spot Santa,
Mrs. Claus, and Reindeer
hidden throughout the story.

To...
You made it onto Santa's NICE list—GOOD JOB!

MERRY CHRISTMAS!

Love, from...

I SAW SANTA IN CALGARY

Written by J.D. Green

Illustrated by Nadja Sarell and Srimalie Bassani

sourcebooks
jabberwocky

anta's not planned his vacation this year.
Mrs. Claus says, "How 'bout Calgary, my dear?
You always say it's your favourite place,
but remember, the children should not see your face."

"It's true," Santa says. "Calgary has it all:
great sights, tasty bites, fun times great and small."

Mrs. Claus says, "We should set off tonight!
And you heard what I said? You must keep out of sight!"

They load up the sleigh, getting set to explore,
and head off to Calgary, ready for more!
Through Fort Calgary, downtown, and Bridgeland they go.
"I love being back!" Santa says. "Ho! Ho! Ho!"

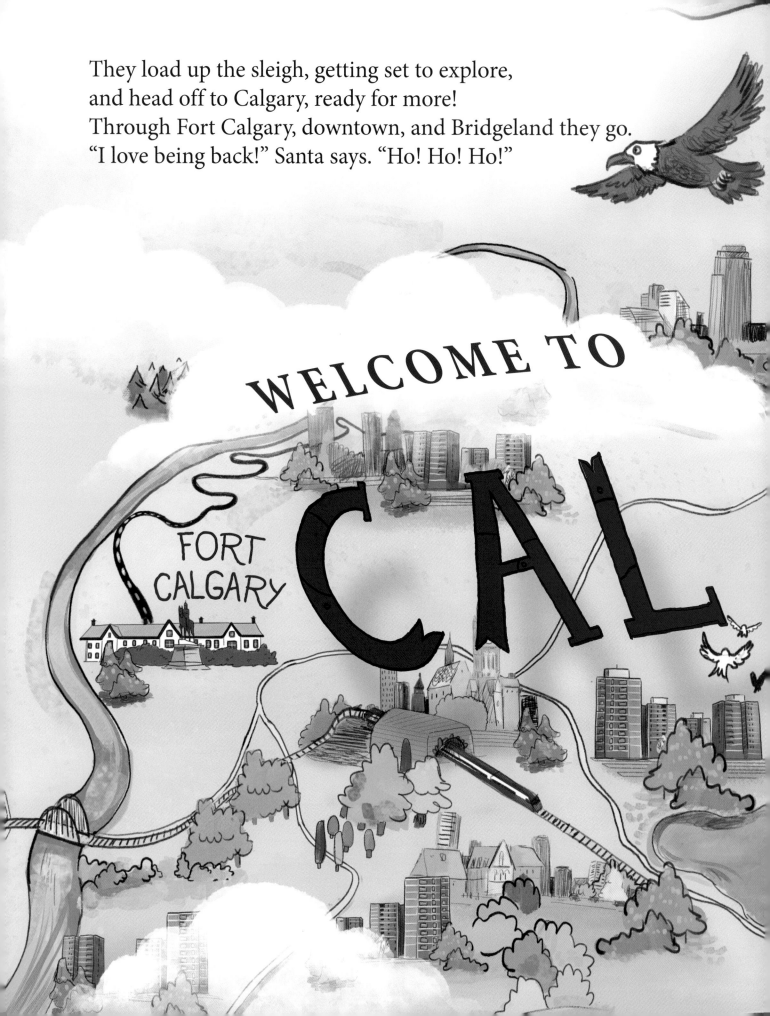

WELCOME TO

CAL

FORT CALGARY

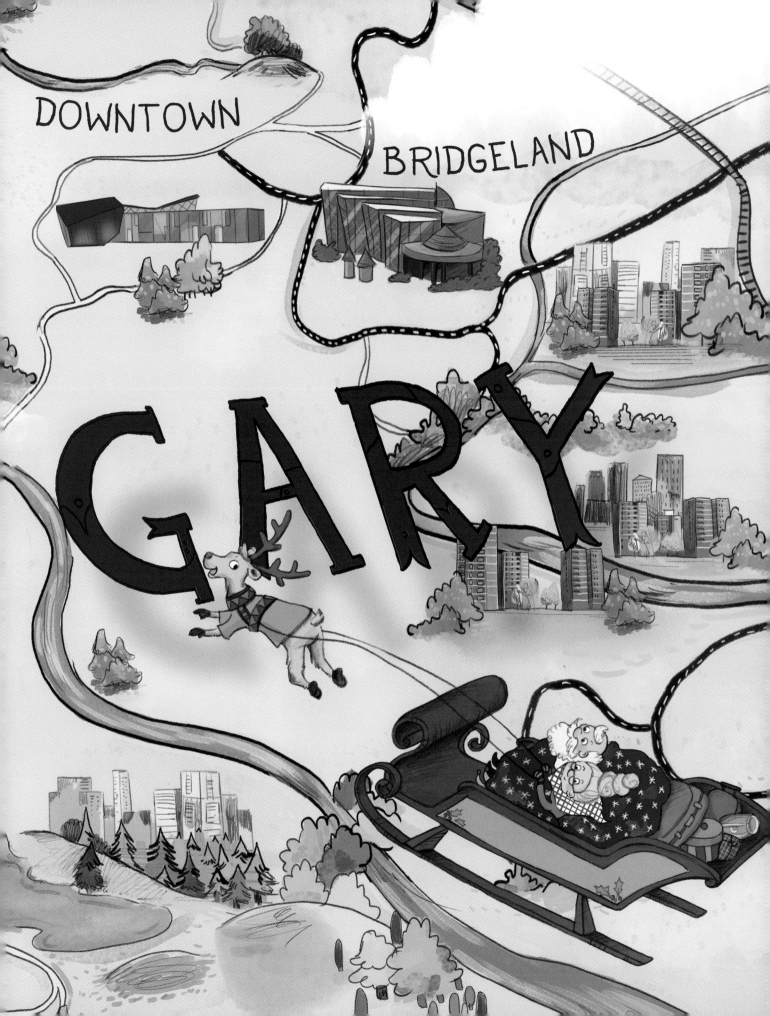

It's a family tradition, when they go away,
to buy a few gifts to remember their stay.

Smart Mrs. Claus came prepared with a list,
so first she'll go shop—not one friend will be missed!

Santa thinks buying nice gifts is quite tough.
He's feeling confused—there's just so much stuff!

His basket fills up with goodies galore, such as ginger beef, pickled carrots, mini donuts, and more.

Reindeer's not eager to stick to plans,
there's so much to see and experience firsthand!

But first he must find a good new disguise,
so he can blend in with the crowd outside!

The Clauses are done with their shopping for friends.
Now it's time to go sightseeing before their trip ends!

Back in the North Pole, Head Elf checks the mail.
He opens one letter and turns very pale…

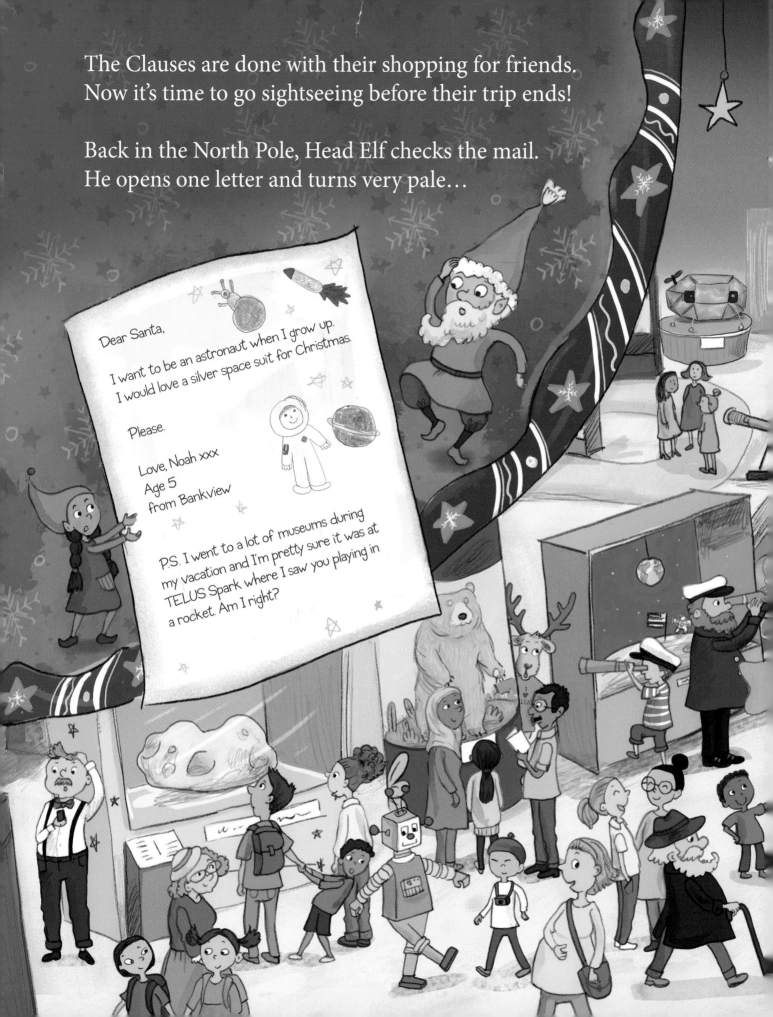

Dear Santa,

I want to be an astronaut when I grow up.
I would love a silver space suit for Christmas.

Please.

Love, Noah xxx
Age 5
from Bankview

P.S. I went to a lot of museums during
my vacation and I'm pretty sure it was at
TELUS Spark where I saw you playing in
a rocket. Am I right?

FREEZE-DRIED
ASTRONAUT ICE CREAM

EXIT

Dear Santa,

My favourite place in the whole wide world is the ocean! Please can I have a snorkel and flippers for Christmas? Thank you!

By the way, I was at Village Square Leisure Centre yesterday. I didn't have my glasses on while I was swimming, but I saw someone with a big, white beard and a red-and-white bathing suit. Was it you? Please write back and tell me.

Love, Emma
Age 7
from Highwood

At home in the North, Head Elf says, "This won't do!
One sighting is terrible. Now we've had two!"

Santa really should be taking more care.
It seems yet more children have spotted him there.

Dear Santa,

I would love, love, love a big, pink unicorn!
I drew one for you here.

Love, Bella x X x
Age 5¾
from Millrise

P.S. Did I see you at Griffith Woods Park,
wearing green hiking boots and a red-and-white
striped backpack? It even sounded like you were
whistling "Neighbours of the World."

Am I right?

GRIFFITH
WOODS
PARK

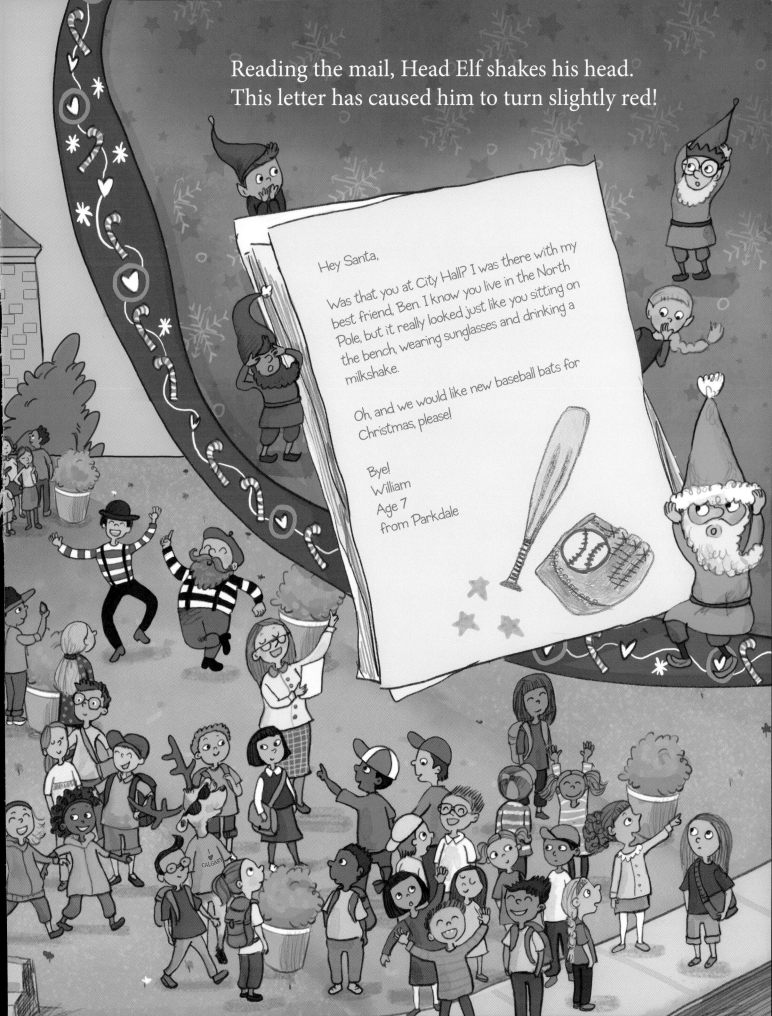

Reading the mail, Head Elf shakes his head.
This letter has caused him to turn slightly red!

Hey Santa,

Was that you at City Hall? I was there with my best friend, Ben. I know you live in the North Pole, but it really looked just like you sitting on the bench, wearing sunglasses and drinking a milkshake.

Oh, and we would like new baseball bats for Christmas, please!

Bye!
William
Age 7
from Parkdale

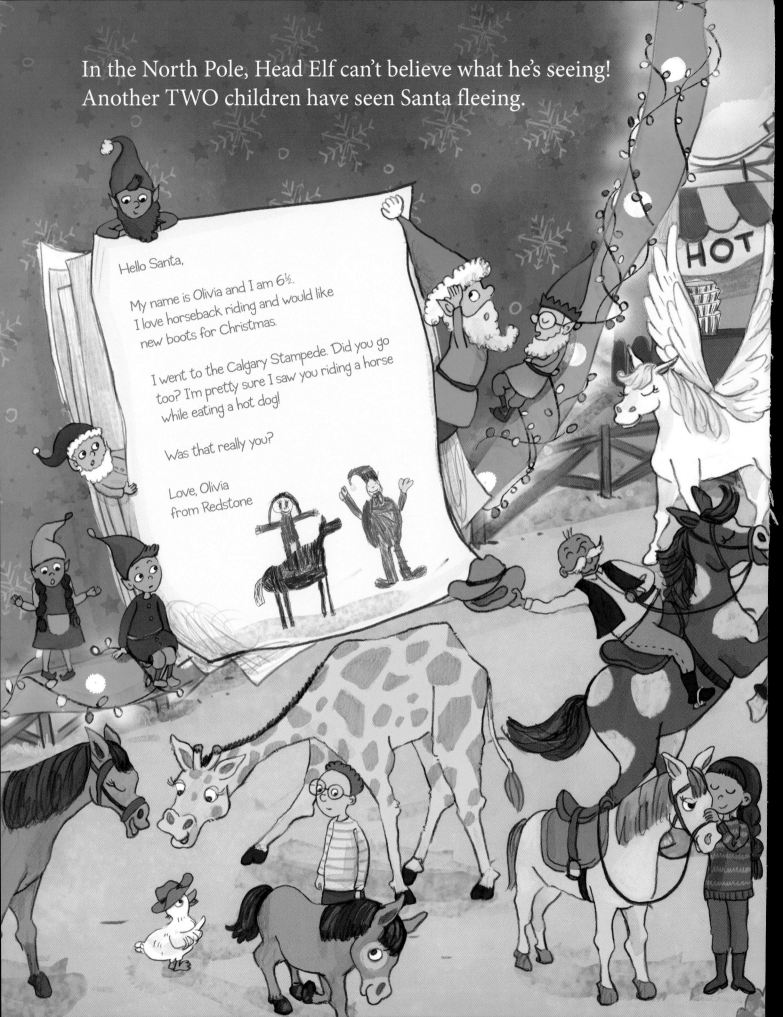

In the North Pole, Head Elf can't believe what he's seeing!
Another TWO children have seen Santa fleeing.

Hello Santa,

My name is Olivia and I am 6½.
I love horseback riding and would like
new boots for Christmas.

I went to the Calgary Stampede. Did you go
too? I'm pretty sure I saw you riding a horse
while eating a hot dog!

Was that really you?

Love, Olivia
from Redstone

HOT

Hi Santa,

I am 8 and I would like a real duck for Christmas. My grandpa and I were watching the ducks at RiverWalk when we saw a big, red sleigh on the other side of the pond. I heard the park ranger say sleighs do not float.

Was that you?

James
from Montgomery

The vacation is over; the shopping is done.
See you soon, Calgary! Thanks for the fun!

Upon arriving home, Head Elf lets Santa know he's been spotted by multiple children. Oh no!

Emma, age 7

Noah, age 5

Bella, age 5¾

Dear Noah,
Yes, you did spot me at TELUS Spark! I was on my summer vacation in Calgary.

Enjoy your silver space suit.

Love, Santa
x

Dear Emma,
Yes, you did spot me at Village Square Leisure Centre! Calgary is my favourite place to visit.
Have fun with your snorkel and flippers.

Love, Santa
x

Dear Bella,
Yes, you did spot me at Griffith Woods Park! I was on my summer vacation in Calgary.
Have fun with your pink unicorn!
Love, Santa
x

Mrs. Claus and Santa know just what to do.
They'll clean up this mess with a special gift or two.

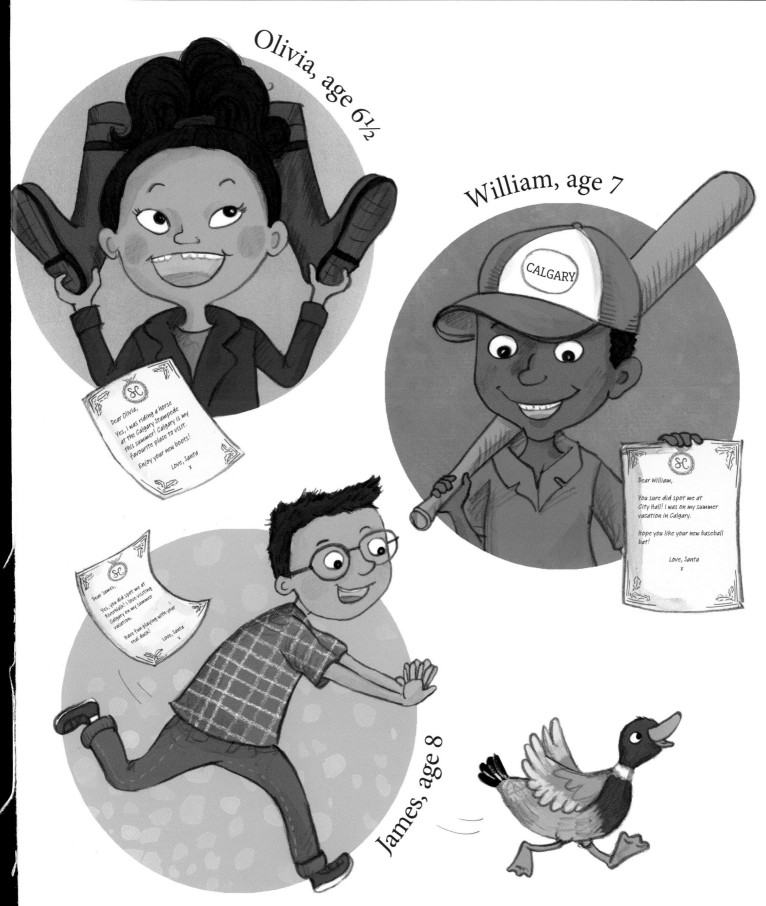

Olivia, age 6½

Dear Olivia,
Yes, I was riding a horse at the Calgary Stampede this summer! Calgary is my favourite place to visit.
Enjoy your new boots!
Love, Santa
x

William, age 7

Dear William,
You sure did spot me at City Hall! I was on my summer vacation in Calgary.
Hope you like your new baseball bat!
Love, Santa
x

Dear James,
Yes, you did spot me at Riverwalk! I love visiting Calgary on my summer vacation.
Have fun playing with your real duck!
Love, Santa
x

James, age 8

When Christmas arrives, all the children who wrote
get one EXTRA gift, and inside is a note…

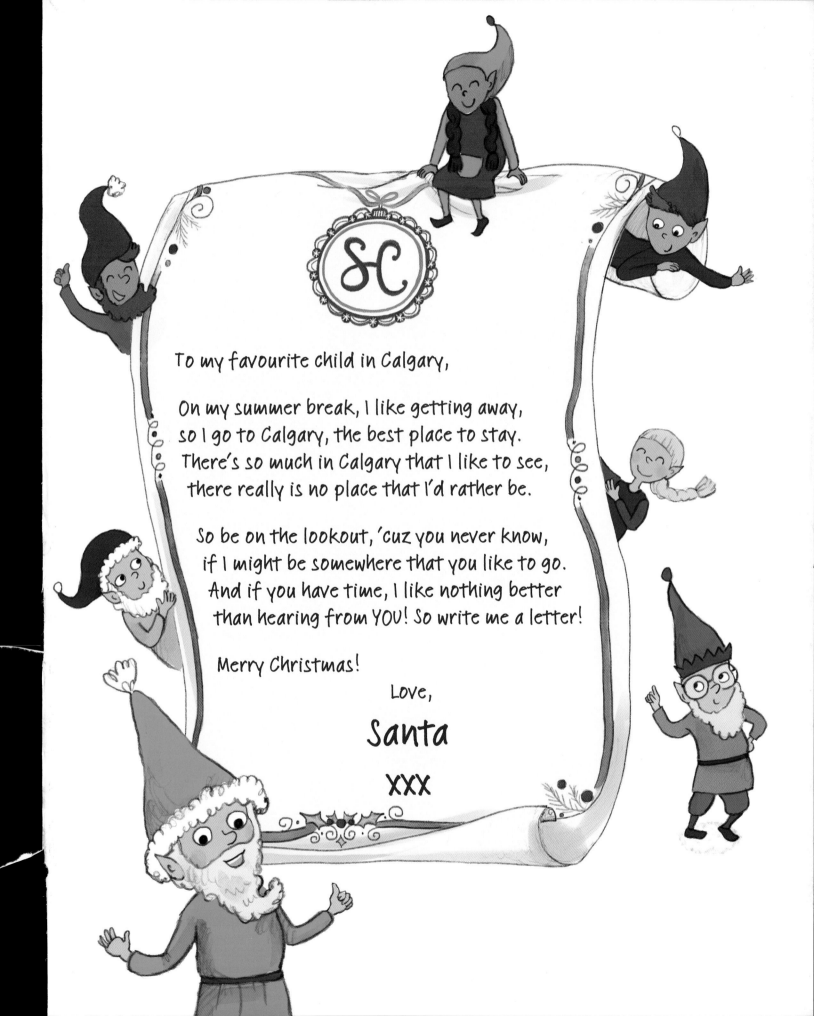

To my favourite child in Calgary,

On my summer break, I like getting away,
so I go to Calgary, the best place to stay.
There's so much in Calgary that I like to see,
there really is no place that I'd rather be.

So be on the lookout, 'cuz you never know,
if I might be somewhere that you like to go.
And if you have time, I like nothing better
than hearing from YOU! So write me a letter!

Merry Christmas!

Love,

Santa

xxx

Written by J.D. Green
Illustrated by Nadja Sarell and Srimalie Bassani
Additional art by Leo Trinidad and Darran Holmes
Designed by Geff Newland

Published by Sourcebooks Jabberwocky, an imprint of Sourcebooks, Inc.
P.O. Box 4410, Naperville, Illinois 60567-4410
(630) 961-3900
Fax: (630) 961-2168
jabberwockykids.com

Date of Production: August 2018
Run Number: HTW_PO201802
Printed and bound in China (GD)
10 9 8 7 6 5 4 3 2 1

Hey, kids! Flick back and see if you can spot Santa,
Mrs. Claus, and Reindeer hidden throughout the story.